STACY *and the*
Greek Festival

Karen Papandrew

Drew Publishing Company

This book is a work of fiction. Names, characters, places and incidents are either products of the author's imagination or are used fictitiously. Any resemblance to actual events or locales or persons, either living or dead, is entirely coincidental.

Published by
Drew Publishing Company
P.O. Box 3158
Sequim, WA 98382

IBSN: 0-9658730-0-5
Library of Congress Card Catalog Number: 97-68236

First printing: August 1997

Cover art by Stephanie Tschida

Printed in the USA

To David,

without whom
I would never
have attended
my first
Greek Festival!

And

to Father Steve

and

all the
YiaYia's
I have ever
known.

STACY and the
Greek Festival

1

"Girls! Please give me your undivided attention," commanded Mrs. Nelson. "I think you'll want to hear what I have to say."

The whispering ceased as fourteen faces turned to watch their scout leader. "School will be over soon, and as a grand finale, I'd like to invite all of you to come to my ranch in the mountains for the weekend. I have lots of horses."

Horses!

Stacy looked up quickly, immediately alert. Had she heard right? Did Mrs. Nelson say she had horses on her ranch? Horses the girl scouts would get to ride?

Mrs. Nelson was moving among the girls and handing each of them a piece of paper. She held it up.

"This contains all the information about the weekend. It's not this coming weekend, but the following one. There's a permission slip at the bottom for your parents to sign, and my telephone number is there so they can call me if they have any questions, or if they'd like to come along and help chaperon."

As the girls collected their books and hurried out of the room, Mrs. Nelson called after them. "I need to get the signed permission slips back by Monday."

"I can't believe it! I just can't believe it!" Stacy danced around Erin, jumping up and down. "It can't be true. Oh, it has to be true!"

"It is, Stace," said Erin, trying to avoid her best friend's overzealous hugs. "You have the invitation in your hand. All we need now is our parents' permission."

"And then it's off to the mountains for a glorious weekend of horseback riding, barbecues, horseback riding, hayrides, and more horseback riding!" exclaimed Stacy. "Oh, Erin, I can hardly wait! Do you realize that I'm ten years old, and I've never even seen a real horse?"

"I don't believe it," said Erin.

"Well, believe it," returned Stacy. "I've had a very deprived childhood."

Stacy loved horses. While most girls her age covered their bedroom walls with posters of their favorite movie, tv, and video stars, Stacy preferred Kentucky Derby winners. Such was her hunger that she even watched old westerns and reruns of *My Friend Flicka*, *Fury*, and *Mr. Ed*. Breed and color were not important. She had the complete set of The Black Stallion Books in her bookcase, and the pure white Lippizaner stallions reared and marched across the quilt that adorned her bed.

Horses made of various materials and in a variety of sizes had specific places of honor on her dresser. And in among the menagerie was Stacy's prized photograph of her great grandmother, Sofia, astride the beautiful gray mare which had been her wedding present from Spiro. The now tattered black and white picture had been taken just outside the church in Sofia's village in southern Greece. Still dressed in her wedding gown, YiaYia Sofia had scandalized the village by riding the horse like a man. And bareback, yet! And married only a few hours! Now at nearly ninety-one, YiaYia Sofia was Stacy's "equine confidant".

"YiaYia!" Stacy called as she raced into the house. "I'm going to ride a horse!"

"Give YiaYia a kiss, Koritzakimou." Stacy bent over the chair and hugged her great grandmother and kissed her soft cheek. "Now tell me about this horse you ride."

"I haven't ridden it yet, YiaYia, but my girl scout leader has invited the whole troop to her ranch in the mountains for the weekend. She has lots of horses, and I'll get to ride one of them!"

Stacy bounced around the room. "Oh, YiaYia, I'm so excited!"

"I would never have guessed." When YiaYia Sofia laughed, her eyes closed and were lost in the wrinkles surrounding them. "Anastasia, dear, I'm laughing so much my hair is falling out. Please pin it back for me."

Stacy hurried to retrieve the bobbypin that was

hanging at the end of a long white curl which had escaped the loose bun at the back of her great grandmother's head. She pushed it back into place. YiaYia Sofia's hair was feather soft and pure white. Sometimes she wore it in the long single braid down her back which was Stacy's favorite style.

"Where's Mama?"

"She's at the church making baklava for the festival. I was just too tired to go today."

Stacy looked closely at her great grandmother. It wasn't like her to miss the comradery of festival baking without a very good reason. But YiaYia Sofia looked okay. Her eyes still had their usual sparkle.

"This is my last festival," YiaYia Sofia said quietly.

"YiaYia, you say that every year!"

"This time I mean it."

"You say that, too."

"Kako koritzi!" YiaYia Sofia shook her finger at Stacy and frowned, pursing her lips into an angry pout. "Go get ready to dance."

Stacy put the permission slip in her jewelry box for safe keeping. She would ask her mother to sign it tonight so she could give it back to Mrs. Nelson on Monday. Seeing the picture of her great grand-mother, Stacy picked it up and gave it a quick kiss. She knew YiaYia Sofia was not really mad at her even though she called her a naughty girl.

"Please don't be too tired to come watch me dance," said Stacy.

She replaced the picture, collected her dance shoes, and went outside to wait for Stephanie's mom to pick her up.

Stacy thought about her great grandmother as she sat on the front step. She could not remember a time when they had not lived with YiaYia Sofia in this house. Mama said that when Papou Spiro had died, Mama's mother had tried to get YiaYia Sofia to move to Arizona and live with her, but YiaYia Sofia did not want to trade her friends and her church for the desert heat. So, when YiaYia Sofia turned seventy-three, Mama went to live with her instead.

"If Mama had stayed in Arizona, she wouldn't have met Papa, and I wouldn't be here," thought Stacy as Stephanie's mother's car pulled into the driveway. Before getting into the back seat, Stacy waved at YiaYia Sofia who was standing at the window, smiling.

Stephanie and Stacy hurried into the upstairs recreation hall of St. Demetrios Greek Orthodox Church. Along the wall was a rack with all the costumes the dancers would wear during the festival.

"Good, now we have everybody here," said Mrs. Pappas, their dance instructor. "Let's get started. Today is Friday, and we have only three more practices before the festival next weekend. Your parents must let you stay after church on Sunday and have you here Tuesday and Thursday evenings at 6:30. Be sure to tell them."

"Can we try on the costumes?" asked Stephanie.

"After practice you will try on the costumes. If

they need any alterations, we can make them by next week. Boys, if the white boots for the Cretan dances are too big, you can stuff newspaper in the toes. Let's go. Places everybody."

There were seven girls and five boys in Stacy's junior dance group. They would do most of the dancing at the Greek Festival this year. Stacy thought it was fun to dress up in the beautiful costumes and whirl around the special dance floor set up outside under the blue and white striped tent. She liked to hear the people clap as she led the group in the line dancing. She was a good dancer. She had been doing it for five years now. But she was not as good as George. He was incredible! He could kick his feet and leap high into the air. And he was only eleven.

After practice, Stephanie, George, and Stacy went into the downstairs hall where their mothers were busy making baklava, the honey and nut pastry most often associated with Greek food. Stacy sat in a chair across the table from her mother.

"The costumes fit perfectly, Mama."

Stacy licked her finger before sticking it into the sugar, cinnamon, and nut mixture and then into her mouth.

"Anastasia!" scolded her mother, whacking the back of Stacy's hand lightly with her buttery paint brush.

Stacy licked the butter off her hand. "Can I help?"

"Only if you will finish a whole pan."

"I will, Mama, I promise. It looks easy."

"Go wash your hands while I set up a place for you."

Stacy's mother handed her a clean paint brush and a foil cake pan. She placed an electric skillet holding the melted butter next to Stacy.

"Now pay attention. Brush the pan with butter. Then take one layer of fillo and put it on the bottom. You need to be very careful, so it doesn't tear. Brush it with butter. Be generous, but not too generous. Then add another layer of fillo. Put eight layers of fillo on the bottom."

Stacy tapped her nose with the paint brush and waved at Stephanie and George as they went into the kitchen.

"Anastasia, are you listening to me?"

Stacy nodded. "Yes, Mama. Not too much butter. Eight pieces."

"Then take a cup of the nut mixture and spread it evenly over the fillo. Do four more layers of fillo. Then another layer of nuts. Then four more layers of fillo," instructed Stacy's mother. "Any questions?"

"How many layers of nuts should there be?"

"Three."

"How many layers of fillo for the top?"

"Ten. And use the best piece for the very top. Okay?"

"Gotcha!"

Mama sighed.

Stacy picked up a piece of the paper thin fillo. It tore.

7

"Gently, Anastasia," said George's mother, as all eyes turned to gaze at Stacy. "Gently."

Stacy swallowed and looked sheepishly at the assembled mothers. "I guess it's not as easy as it looks," she admitted.

2

"I made a whole pan by myself," announced Stacy, bounding into the living room and waking YiaYia Sofia. She hugged her great grandmother. "Didn't I, Mama?"

"It will be the first pan sold at the festival," said Mama, kissing YiaYia Sofia's cheek. "How are you feeling now?"

"How am I supposed to feel, Eleni? I'm an old lady. I feel old."

"It's nice to know nothing's changed, YiaYia," said Mama, laughing and yawning at the same time. "All your friends asked about you. You'd better go tomorrow or you'll miss all the gossip."

"We don't gossip."

"What do you call it then?" asked Mama.

"We talk."

Mama shook her head and sighed. "My back hurts. We made two hundred pans of baklava today." Mama stretched and rolled her head slowly from side to side.

"I made one," declared Stacy.

"You'll have to do better than that next year," said Mama.

"Your mama's right. I may be gone and you'll have to do my share next year."

"YiaYia, don't say that," cried Stacy.

"I'm over ninety, and I could go at any time."

"Anastasia took two hours to make one pan of baklava," said Mama. "We are going to need your help for a long time, so don't plan on falling asleep in the Lord's arms just yet."

Mama shook her finger at YiaYia.

"Besides, your mother lived to be a hundred and twelve. And she would've lived longer if she hadn't fallen out of the cherry tree!"

Stacy gasped. "Great, great grandmother Eleni fell out of a cherry tree when she was a hundred and twelve?"

"She said the men were too slow coming back from the kafeneon, and she wanted to get started on her vassinada. She made the best cherry jam of anyone in our village," explained YiaYia Sofia. "But when she fell out of the tree, she broke her hip and had to stay in bed. Since she couldn't get around anymore, she asked the Savior to come and get her. And He did."

"Oh, my gosh," whispered Stacy.

YiaYia Sofia patted her chest proudly. "My mother was something special. The villagers said I took after her. Especially when I rode Spiro's mare bareback through the village on our wedding day. Ha ha! That was such fun! My hair was flying." She reached behind her head and touched her hair. "Of course, it was darker then." She tapped her chin. "As I remember, I nearly ran over the priest," mused YiaYia Sofia with a laugh. "That was some horse!"

"Horse!" cried Stacy as she raced for her room. She snatched the invitation from its hiding place and hurried back into the living room. She handed the slip to her mother. "I almost forgot!"

"What is it?" asked Mama.

"Mrs. Nelson invited the whole girl scout troop to her ranch in the mountains for the weekend. She has horses and everything. Can I go, Mama? Please, can I go?" Stacy pleaded.

"And is Mrs. Nelson going to watch over fourteen ten year old girls for a whole weekend by herself? Where will you sleep?"

"Mrs. Nelson has a bunkhouse."

"A bunk house?" asked YiaYia. "Ti enay ena bunk house?"

Mama thought for a moment. "Enas ipno-thalamos. A dormitory. With beds stacked on top of each other. Only for cowboys."

"They all sleep together in the same room?" asked YiaYia Sofia.

Mama nodded.

"Are there any mothers going? How will you get there?" asked Mama.

"Read the invitation. It tells everything, Mama."

Stacy waited anxiously while her mother scanned the paper. Mama looked up, but before she could get any words from her open mouth, Stacy slid to her knees.

"Please, Mama. I've always dreamed of riding a horse, and now it could come true," she begged. "Please, please, please. Can I go?"

"Get up. You look silly," said Mama reaching down and pulling Stacy to her feet. "I'll think about it. I'll have to talk to your father. You don't need to return this until Monday, so we'll decide by then."

"Oh, thank you, Mama," squealed Stacy, hugging her mother tightly. "Thank you, thank you."

"Don't get your hopes up, young lady. I haven't said yes."

"But you didn't say no!"

"Kiss us good night and go to bed. It's late."

Stacy hugged and kissed Mama and YiaYia Sofia and hurried to her room humming *"Home on the Range."*

"Horses! Why can't she be interested in dolls, clothes, or movie stars? Why horses?"

"Because she is so much like me," said YiaYia Sofia. "I think it's a nice thing for the lady to do. Kosta won't mind, will he?"

"Of course not. He'll be busy at the restaurant. He won't even know she's gone."

"Then why do you look so unhappy?"

Mama sighed.

"This weekend with the horses is the same weekend as the Greek Festival."

3

Stacy dressed quickly and hurried into the kitchen. YiaYia Sofia was standing at the sink washing dishes. As she hummed one of the songs from her village, YiaYia Sofia's feet shuffled the dance steps. Wash a dish, shuffle right, kick, dish into the strainer, shuffle left to sink, kick.

"You're good, YiaYia. Why don't you come be in my dance group?" asked Stacy, fumbling in the pantry for the cereal.

"Too old," said YiaYia Sofia. "I'll leave the water. Wash your dish when you're through."

"That's okay. I'll just put it in the dishwasher."

"Whoosh! Whoosh! Whoosh!" complained Yia-Yia Sofia. "Is not good for the dishes. Better to wash them in the sink."

"Okay," said Stacy. "Is Mama at the restaurant?"

YiaYia Sofia nodded. Mama always helped Papa on Saturdays. That was the busiest day, especially for breakfast and lunch. Sunday was busy too, but Mama always went to church first. Since the restaurant was open every day for all three meals, Stacy didn't see her father very often. He went there to open in the morning and stayed there to close at night. But he did name the restaurant for her. Well, sort of. He open-ed it soon after she was born and called it 'Papa's Place'. Stacy figured he wouldn't have been a Papa if it hadn't been for her, and she wanted to get big enough to work there. Maybe this summer he would allow her to help in the kitchen, peeling carrots and potatoes or washing dishes. She might even get to bus the tables.

"Did Mama talk to Papa yet?" asked Stacy, following YiaYia around as she straightened and dusted the furniture.

"I don't know," she answered. "I was sleeping when they left this morning."

"They'll let me go, don't you think?" Stacy took YiaYia Sofia's hands in hers and danced with her around the room. "It will be so much fun."

YiaYia Sofia sat down in the armchair next to the couch. "Pedakimou, you have too much energy for me," she said, picking up a nearby magazine and fanning her face.

"YiaYia, what was it like to have your own horse? Weren't you excited?"

"My little village in Greece was full of very poor people. A donkey to help with the harvest was a real blessing. But to own a horse!" YiaYia Sofia's eyes sparkled. "Your Papou Spiro chose me for his bride when I was just sixteen, but we couldn't get married right away. Times were hard in Greece so Spiro went away to America to make his fortune. He did not come back for three years. But when he did, he brought me such a horse for a wedding gift."

"And you rode it through the village on your wedding day."

"I embarrassed your Papou," admitted YiaYia Sofia. "But you know, Pedakimou, it was the most fun!" She leaned close to Stacy and whispered, "Your Papou locked me in the house for a week."

YiaYia Sofia laughed at the memory and tears rolled down her cheeks. "Your Papou was such a good man."

"I wish I could've known him."

"Me too, Koritzimou."

Stacy had heard the story of her great grand-mother's wedding many times, but somehow every telling seemed different. Papou Spiro had died when he was sixty-five and YiaYia Sofia was only sixty. She had lived alone for thirteen years in the house he built for her before Mama came to live with her. Stacy knew him only from a very few old pictures and the stories in YiaYia Sofia's memory.

"I'm going over to Erin's house for awhile," said Stacy. "I'll be back for lunch. Okay?"

"Of course. Why should you want to stay and keep an old lady company?"

"YiaYia!"

"Go!" YiaYia Sofia laughed, making shooing motions with her hands, and chased Stacy out of the house. She tapped her left wrist. "Thotheka ora, Anastasia!"

"I'll be back at twelve o'clock sharp," called

Stacy and headed down the street.

Erin answered Stacy's knock and led them into her bedroom.

"My aunt sent me a new dress for my birthday," said Erin. "Want to see it?"

"Your birthday's not until next month," said Stacy.

Erin shrugged. "She never remembers it right. She always gets Eric's and my birthdays confused. Eric will be twelve tomorrow."

"Then he'll get his present next month."

The girls giggled as Erin pulled the dress over her head and turned to let Stacy zip the zipper. The light green flowered print made Erin's hair look even redder than usual.

"It's really pretty," said Stacy. "It's perfect for you."

"You want to try it on?"

"Nah. With this mass of dark hair and bushy eyebrows, I'd look horrible in it." Stacy combed her fingers through her hair. "My hair is so thick and curly. I wish it was long and straight so I could braid it like my great grandmother's."

"At least yours is naturally curly. And your mom doesn't force you to get a permanent every summer just before school starts like mine does," said Erin, shaking her head.

Erin's fine, thin hair hung in ringlets just touching her shoulders. She looked at herself in the mirror.

"I hope Mom will let me have my hair long this

year," said Erin wistfully as she changed into her jeans and t-shirt and put the dress back in her closet.

"Did you ask your folks about the scout trip?" asked Stacy.

Erin opened her purse and pulled out the permission slip. "Signed and ready for delivery Monday," she said, waving it in Stacy's face. "How about yours?"

"Mama has to talk to Papa. He'll be at the restaurant all weekend, so I won't know until Monday morning," Stacy explained. "The suspense is killing me!"

She fell backwards onto Erin's bed with her hands crossed over her chest, then sat up quickly.

"But they haven't said I can't," she stated. "Let's go over to Randall's drugstore. I need something chocolate!"

"That'll just make your face break out," declared Erin, giggling.

"Not me," said Stacy. "I'm too young."

Erin examined her face closely in the mirror.

"Those are just freckles, Erin," said Stacy, dragging her friend out the door. "Come on. I promised my great grandmother I'd be home at twelve for lunch."

4

The clock on the mantle over the fireplace counted out the twelfth hour as Stacy pushed open the back door. She expected to see YiaYia Sofia standing at the kitchen table, pan and soup ladle in hand, but she wasn't there. The table wasn't set for lunch either.

"YiaYia," she called.

There was no answer. Stacy felt her heartbeat quicken as she hurried through the house. The door to YiaYia Sofia's room was closed.

"That's strange," thought Stacy as she knocked softly. When her great grandmother didn't respond, Stacy turned the doorknob and pushed the door open slowly.

YiaYia Sofia was sitting in her rocking chair. The old chest she had brought from Greece nearly seventy years ago was open and its contents were spread carefully upon the bed. In her lap were two rings of dried flowers tied together with a long ribbon that had once been white. She was staring at the far wall. The squeak of the rocking chair as it moved slowly back and forth was the only sound in the room.

"YiaYia, are you okay?" whispered Stacy.

She licked her lips and swallowed hard. Her heart was beating very fast. She tiptoed across the room and knelt beside the rocking chair.

"YiaYia?"

Tears were rolling slowly down her great grandmother's cheeks. Stacy bit at her lower lip to keep from crying.

"YiaYia, what's wrong?"

Stacy picked up YiaYia Sofia's right hand and held it in both of hers. She touched the gold band on YiaYia Sofia's third finger. Stacy remembered asking her why she and Mama wore their wedding rings on their right hands while Erin's mother wore her ring on her left hand.

"It is the hand of honor," YiaYia Sofia had answered, and Stacy had never seen this hand without the wedding ring. She looked up quickly as YiaYia Sofia took her hand away and cupped it under Stacy's chin.

"Signomi, Korizakimou. I'm sorry. I was lost in the past."

Stacy let out the breath she was holding. "Boy, YiaYia, you sure had me scared," she admonished, her voice shaking. "Are you okay?"

YiaYia Sofia nodded. Stacy picked up the dried flower rings. "What are these?"

"That is the stephana from my wedding," said YiaYia Sofia, taking them from Stacy. "These were once fresh flowers."

She smiled, sniffed, and brushed away the wetness from her cheeks.

"It is the most beautiful part of the ceremony. The priest holds the stephana and he crowns the bride to the groom and then the groom to the bride three times. Like so."

YiaYia Sofia held the two crowns together carefully in her right hand, the ribbon flowing loose in her lap. She touched the upright ring lightly to Stacy's forehead.

"He would chant 'the handmaiden of God, Anastasia, is crowned to the servant of God, George.'"

"YiaYia! Not George!"

YiaYia Sofia laughed. "Then the koumbara places the crowns on their heads, exchanging them three times, and the priest leads them in the dance of Isaiah around the wedding table while the koumbara holds the ribbon." YiaYia Sofia's eyes sparkled. "Poli oraya. Very beautiful!"

"Did you always know you were going to marry Papou Spiro?"

"Oh, no. I had only seen him once before we were betrothed."

Stacy's eyes opened as wide as her mouth. "You mean you didn't date or anything?"

YiaYia Sofia closed her eyes and sighed. "No, Anastasia, things were very different in Greece then. Marriages were arranged by the families.

"It was two years after the great war ended.

Your Papou Spiro was twenty-one when he came to help shear the sheep for his cousin whose husband had broken his leg. He was only in our village a few days, but there was fire in our hearts when we first saw each other. We didn't speak. That would not have been allowed, but oh what lightning passed between us!" YiaYia clasped her hand to her heart, closed her eyes, and sighed.

"Go on, YiaYia."

"He finished the work and went back to his village. The next thing I knew his family had sent someone to speak to my family, and the dowry was decided."

"What's a dowry?"

"That's what the bride's family gives the groom. A rich bride brings her husband a large dowry and much respect."

"Is a dowry money?"

"Sometimes. In the city it might be a house. In my village a rich bride would bring land to build a house and fields to plant. Sheep and goats. Maybe a donkey."

"What was your dowry, YiaYia?"

"Not much. We were very poor."

"Will I have a dowry when I get married?"

"No, Anastasia. In America it is enough that you and your husband love each other. Besides, your father will spend plenty on your wedding party!"

Stacy giggled. "Then what happened?"

YiaYia Sofia had never told her this part of the story before.

"Times were hard in the villages. Prices were high and food was scarce. The government kept changing. Spiro's family postponed the marriage so he could go to Canada and live with a cousin in Vancouver. When Spiro was able to, he moved to America. He got a job cutting trees in Washington, and when he had earned enough money, he came back to Greece."

YiaYia Sofia stood up and began to gather the items on the bed and return them to the chest.

"I kept all my linens for our marriage in this chest. It was my mother's and her mother's before her. It is very old." She ran her finger over the carved wood. There were many scratches on the lid.

"Did Papou Spiro bring the horse with him?"

"Yes, he wanted to show my family that he was rich and a worthy son-in-law. We were married in 1921. And such a wedding feast you've never seen! Everybody came. The people followed us from my family's house after the betrothal ceremony and filled the little church. Afterwards there was much dancing. The tables bent from the weight of the food. And of course, we had plenty of wine. There were so many toasts to the bride and groom. It took all day!"

YiaYia Sofia sat on the edge of the bed and fingered the lace on a worn pillowcase. "Ah, so much to remember."

"Why did you come to America instead of staying in your village?"

"Life was not good in Greece. King Constantine

came back after King Alexander died. Then Greece invaded Turkey and lost, and King Constantine left again and his son King George II came. Almost two million Greeks living in Turkey were returned to Greece. There was no place for all of them. No food, no houses, no jobs. When King George left the country, Spiro decided we should go, too."

YiaYia Sofia continued to repack the chest. Stacy listened intently. YiaYia Sofia had never talked about this part of her life before.

"I didn't want to leave my parents. Your YiaYia Kalliope was just a baby. But your Papou Spiro was determined to get back to Washington before America changed the immigration quotas again. There was no life for us in the village. I could either stay in Greece without Spiro or go with him to a country I knew nothing about. He promised he would send for our families as soon as he could."

YiaYia Sofia turned to face Stacy. "Of course, we came and we were able to bring the families over, too, but that was the hardest decision I ever made in my life."

"What about your horse?" asked Stacy. She was sitting in the middle of YiaYia Sofia's bed.

"We had to sell her to pay for the passage to America for the three of us," said YiaYia Sofia.

The lid of the chest fell shut with a bang.

5

Stacy sat between Mama and YiaYia Sofia in the fourth row from the front on the south side of the church. YiaYia Sofia liked to sit next to the aisle so she could see and hear Father Nick. Sometimes Stacy wondered what it would be like to sit upstairs or maybe in the front row. But Mama always said, "This is where we sit."

Stacy's mind wandered. "I wonder if Mrs. Nelson has a gray mare like YiaYia's," she thought, a smile spreading over her face. "I'd like to ride it bareback."

Mama pinched her. Everyone was standing for the reading of the Gospel. Stacy stood up quickly and listened as Father Nick read in his strong, booming voice. He was a big man, and his robes made him seem even bigger. There were gray streaks in his dark hair and beard. She liked Father Nick. Everybody did.

Stacy closed her eyes. She could see Father Nick riding through her great grandmother's village on a big black horse. He was wearing his green robes and carrying the jeweled Gospel book. The people were following him to the church. YiaYia Sofia was there in the crowd, and so was Stacy. Suddenly Father Nick stopped his horse in front of her. Stacy reached up to him. She wanted to ride the big horse, too. As Father Nick leaned over to lift her up, YiaYia Sofia pulled her away and shook her.

Stacy woke up and rubbed her eyes. YiaYia Sofia really was shaking her, but she was no longer in her YiaYia's village. The church service was over.

"Come downstairs when you're through with practice," instructed Mama, as they filed out of the church. Stacy kissed Father Nick's hand as he gave her a piece of antidoron, the blessed bread.

Stacy raced ahead of her mother to join Stephanie, and after greeting each other with a hug, the two girls headed into the hall. Mrs. Pappas was already there.

"Change your shoes," she said. "Hurry up. We don't have much time."

Stacy figured she had lots of time. Mama and YiaYia Sofia would be talking with their friends for at least an hour. Church was for prayer and worship, but after church was for gossip.

They rehearsed the first dance three times before Mrs. Pappas pronounced them good enough to go on to the next one. There were moans of discontent as they began the last dance for the fifth time.

"Can't we stop now?" asked Stephanie. "We're tired."

"You'd better build up your stamina," warned Mrs. Pappas, as she dismissed the group. "You have to dance twice on Friday, four times on Saturday, and four times on Sunday."

Mama was helping YiaYia Sofia up the stairs as Stacy started down. "Your father needs me at the restaurant," she said. "Stay with YiaYia while I bring the car around to the door. She's not feeling well."

Mama was gone all afternoon. Stacy had planned to go over to Erin's house, but Mama didn't want YiaYia Sofia to be alone, so she stayed home. When YiaYia Sofia laid down on the couch, Stacy covered her with the quilt from her bed.

"Will you read to me for awhile?" asked YiaYia Sofia.

"Sure," answered Stacy, hurrying to her room for the book they had been reading together. She sat on the floor beside the couch and opened the book to chapter sixteen and began to read aloud.

"You are reading so much better," complimented YiaYia Sofia. "Every time, so much better."

"Thank you, YiaYia."

"Now I feel when you read you become the boy in the book," said YiaYia Sofia. "Is good."

Stacy finished the eighteenth chapter and shut the book. She was thirsty.

"Do you want something to drink, YiaYia?"

"Some tea would be nice, Koritzakimou."

When Stacy returned with the steaming cup, YiaYia Sofia sat up. "You should be out playing with your friends. Not sitting here with an old woman."

"It's okay, YiaYia. I like to read to you."

"These old eyes don't see so well anymore. The letters are too small," complained YiaYia Sofia, snuggling back under the quilt.

She laughed softly. "You know, Anastasia. I learned to read English with your grandmother. When your Papou came back to Greece, he spoke English pretty good, but I was too stubborn to learn the words. I thought 'When will I ever speak English?'"

YiaYia Sofia sat up. "Then we come to America, and I can't speak a word to anybody. Thank goodness for the church. I could talk to people there in Greek, and of course, Spiro and I spoke Greek at home. But poor Kalliope. On the first day I sent her to school, she came home crying. She couldn't speak English, and the other children made fun of her. That's when we both sat down with her reading books and learned English together. I still have an accent, but..."

"I like your accent, YiaYia," said Stacy, kissing her cheek. "And I like your stories. Reading for stories is a fair trade."

Stacy wandered around the room.

"Why don't you invite Erin to come here?" asked YiaYia Sofia.

"She couldn't. Today's her brother's birthday. We were going to crash his party."

YiaYia Sofia looked puzzled. "What means

27

'crash his party'?"

Stacy giggled mischievously. "I'm sorry YiaYia. Erin and I weren't invited to Eric's party, but we were going to go anyway. Sort of as a surprise."

"Ahhh," whispered YiaYia Sofia, nodding her head. "I understand. So now that you can't, uh, crunch the party, will Erin be disappointed with you?"

"Nah."

"Perhaps you could invite her and her brother to the festival?"

"They wouldn't be interested."

"Why not?"

"They just wouldn't be, that's all."

"They would not enjoy the music and the dancing and the food?"

"It's just too different for them. They're American, not Greek," said Stacy. "I don't mix my church friends with my school friends. I don't want what happened to YiaYia Kalliope to happen to me."

YiaYia Sofia shook her head, a bewildered look on her face. Stacy knew she wouldn't understand. None of Stacy's friends from school went to St. Demetrios, and she didn't discuss her church activities with them. She was afraid they would laugh if they came to the festival and saw her and her friends in their costumes dancing such strange dances. It wasn't the way the American kids dressed for a dance. And it certainly wasn't the way they danced!

Stacy heard the car pull into the driveway and ran

to the window. "It's Mama," she called. "I hope she's talked with Papa."

Stacy opened the back door for her mother whose hands were full of boxes. "I brought dinner for you. We are going to be very busy tonight, so I have to go back in a little while."

"Did you talk to Papa?" asked Stacy, lifting the box lid and peeking inside. It was chicken. The fragrant mixture of lemon and garlic filled the room.

"Anastasia, come with me," said Mama, leading her into the living room. Mama kissed YiaYia Sofia's cheek and sat down in the chair. "This is not easy for me."

"What do you mean, Mama?"

"The weekend of this scout trip is the same weekend as the festival," Mama explained. "You can't go."

Stacy looked bewildered. "But Mama, it can't be. Mrs. Nelson said it wasn't this coming weekend. It's the following one. That means it's after the festival."

"No, Pedakimou," said Mama, pulling the invitation out of her pocket. "It has the dates right here."

Stacy took the invitation from her mother's hand. She couldn't read it through the tears gathering in her eyes.

"It was Friday when Mrs. Nelson told you that," explained Mama. "She meant this coming weekend to be yesterday and today and the following one to be next weekend. The weekend of the festival."

Stacy's chin quivered, and tears slid down her cheeks.

"You are the best dancer in the junior group. Mrs. Pappas is counting on you," said Mama, putting her arms around Stacy.

"But I want to go to the mountains!" Stacy pulled away from her mother. "I may never get another chance to ride a horse! I can always dance at the festival next year."

"But I want to see you dance," interjected YiaYia Sofia. "And I may not live another year."

"That's a mean thing to say, YiaYia! Your mother lived to be a hundred and twelve. You're going to live a long time, so don't say that to me ever again!"

Stacy raced from the room to her bedroom, crying hysterically. She slammed the door and stared at the festival poster taped to it.

"I hate you!" she screamed at the poster, ripping it off the door and tearing it to pieces. Sobbing, she dove onto the bed and buried her head in her arms.

Knocking softly, Mama opened the door. "Please don't be angry with YiaYia. She loves you very much. And when you dance, you give her a chance to relive her own youth. For YiaYia, the festival is special. She is full of pride for you. It will break her heart if she can't boast about your dancing at the festival to her friends."

"What about my heart?"

Mama sat on the bed beside Stacy and stroked her hair.

"I know you think you'll never have another chance to ride, but you are still very young. And miracles do happen. The offer will come again."

"No it won't," Stacy wailed. "Oh, Mama, I can dance for YiaYia anytime."

"That's not the point. You are part of a group that needs you. Do you want to let them down?"

"Stephanie can dance my part," whimpered Stacy. "I'm part of the scout troop, too."

Mama looked thoughtful. "That's true, you are. But would you be letting the scout troop down if you didn't go or just yourself?"

Stacy squirmed under her mother's gaze. "I'm ten years old, and I should get to decide what I want to do."

Mama's head tilted to one side as she studied the crumpled pieces of the festival poster lying on the floor. Without a sound, she stood up and walked over to Stacy's desk. Reaching for a pen, she spread the permission slip out flat and signed it. She turned and handed it to Stacy.

"You're right, Anastasia. This decision should be yours."

6

Stacy cut the signed permission slip from the invitation, folded it carefully, and put it in her purse. Scooping up her school books, she hurried into the kitchen. Mama was sitting at the table drinking a cup of Greek coffee.

YiaYia Sofia stood by the stove holding the handle of the briki as she measured coffee and sugar into the water. As the coffee began to boil, it formed a light colored froth on top. Stacy watched YiaYia Sofia pour a small portion of the kaimaki into a delicate china cup and then set the briki back on the burner to boil again. More of the thick dark liquid was added to the cup. After bringing the mixture to a boil for the third time, YiaYia Sofia filled her cup and sat down across from Mama. She took a sip and sighed contentedly.

"Kalos kafes."

"Here's the information on the scout trip," said Stacy, attaching it to the front of the refrigerator with a magnet.

"So you have decided to ride horses instead of

dance at the festival," sighed Mama.

There was no sign of anger on Mama's face, but Stacy could tell she wasn't happy either. Stacy tried to swallow the lump in her throat and stared at the floor, tracing the pattern in the linoleum with her right foot.

"Yes Mama."

"So be it." Mama forced a weak smile. "I hope you have a good time."

"What's this?" asked YiaYia Sofia, looking from Mama to Stacy. "What's going on?"

"I want to go on the scout trip, YiaYia," said Stacy. "Mama said I could choose."

"But..."

Mama held up her hand. She frowned at YiaYia Sofia and shook her head quickly.

"No, YiaYia. Anastasia has made her decision. We're not going to try to change her mind."

"You're not going to dance?" asked YiaYia Sofia, as Stacy bent to kiss her cheek.

"Please don't look so sad, YiaYia. I'll dance next year."

YiaYia Sofia stood up and took the coffee cups to the sink. As she started out the door, she placed her right hand over her heart.

"I don't feel so good. I think I'll go lie down for awhile."

"YiaYia isn't really sick, is she, Mama?"

"No, Anastasia. Just disappointed."

"Mama, there will be lots of festivals for me to dance in, but this may be my only chance to ride a horse. It's my dream come true. Please make YiaYia understand," pleaded Stacy, hugging her mother.

Mama smiled and ran her hand through Stacy's hair. She pushed a loose strand out of Stacy's face.

"Come, you're going to be late for school."

Mama handed Stacy a sack containing her lunch and walked with her down the sidewalk. She kissed Stacy's forehead.

"I'll talk to YiaYia."

"Thanks, Mama," said Stacy, starting down the street. She turned and ran back. "Will you tell Mrs. Pappas, too?"

A stern look came over Mama's face, and she crossed her arms.

"That I won't do. This is your decision, Anastasia. You must explain to Mrs. Pappas why you won't dance at the festival."

Stacy walked slowly to school. She decided she would tell Mrs. Pappas at dance practice tomorrow evening. She hurried to find Erin and tell her the good news. At least Erin would be happy that she was going on the scout trip. Her mother and great grandmother certainly weren't. What was so important about the festival anyway? The church had one every year. And whether she danced or not wouldn't keep YiaYia from going and pretending she was in her village in Greece.

"Hey Stace!" called Erin, running to catch up with her. "You look lost."

"I was just thinking."

"About what?"

"This," said Stacy, taking the permission slip from her purse. "I can go."

"That's great!" squealed Erin, digging through her purse. She matched Stacy's paper with her own. "We're going to have so much fun. Let's go find Mrs. Nelson and give them to her."

Erin raced toward the playground.

"If we're going to have so much fun, how come I'm not as excited as Erin," thought Stacy, trailing after her.

Tuesday was Mama's turn to drive for dance practice. Stacy slid across the back seat to make room for Stephanie. Mama dropped them off at the hall and went to park the car.

"Is your mom staying to make more tsurekia?" asked Stephanie, pointing to the braided sweet breads that were laying in trays on the tables in the downstairs hall.

"They're not going to make more tonight. Just bag these," explained Stacy, taking a deep breath. "Ummm. They smell so good."

"Wow! There are hundreds of them!" grinned Stephanie. "Think they'd miss one?"

Stacy laughed. "Probably. Mama says they have them counted."

"Darn."

George's mother saw them and pointed her finger toward the ceiling. "The dancing is upstairs, girls."

The upstairs hall was full of dancers. All three groups were there to practice. Mrs. Pappas was checking the costumes and talking to Panos Lotakis, the president of the parish council and Stacy's Godfather. Stacy didn't want to interrupt, so she put on her shoes and joined her dance group.

Mrs. Pappas clapped her hands as loud as she could.

"Give me your attention!"

When everyone in the room finally became quiet, she continued.

"At Thursday's practice, Mr. Samuel Cain, a photographer from the newspaper, is coming to take pictures. I want all of you to come as soon after school as you can and get into your costumes. We will make this a dress rehearsal as well. I especially want Anastasia from the junior group for an individual picture."

Stacy gasped. "Mrs. Pappas," she said, raising her hand.

"Yes, Anastasia?"

Stacy squirmed as everyone turned to look at her. How could she tell Mrs. Pappas she couldn't dance at the festival in front of all the other dancers?

"Why me?" she asked.

"You are the most photogenic in the costume," said Mrs. Pappas. Coming close to Stacy, she whispered, "You're also the prettiest."

Stacy's cheeks turned pink, and she looked down at her shoes. "Thank you, Mrs. Pappas."

Mrs. Pappas divided the groups, sending them to different rooms to practice. She kept the junior group in the hall and turned on the music.

"Okay. Let's get started."

Stacy tried two more times to get Mrs. Pappas alone so she could tell her she wouldn't be at the festival, but someone always interrupted. Panos needed Mrs. Pappas to point out on the map where she wanted the speakers and the microphone placed for the festival. And the instructor for the beginner group wanted Mrs. Pappas to show them a new dance step to go with their music. Stacy was frustrated. When George's mother cornered Mrs. Pappas before she could get to her, Stacy gave up and left the hall with Stephanie to find Mama.

Mama put the last loaf of bread into a bag. She held the open end to her mouth and sucked the air out before tying it shut.

"That makes three hundred and twelve loaves."

"Mama, you look tired."

"I am, Anastasia." Mama yawned. "Are you two ready to go home?"

They nodded.

Stacy hurried into the house and changed into her pajamas.

"Mrs. Pappas announced that someone from the newspaper is going to come Thursday to take pictures," explained Stacy to Mama and YiaYia Sofia as they sat at the kitchen table having hot chocolate. "She wants them to take one of just me in my costume because she says I'm the prettiest."

"Did you tell her you won't be dancing at the festival?" asked Mama.

"I didn't get a chance," said Stacy, trying to trap

her marshmallow against the side of the cup. "I'll tell her on Thursday after the man from the newspaper takes the pictures."

"Anastasia, if you're not going to dance, you can't have your picture in the paper."

"Why not?"

"Because people will come expecting to see you, and you will not be there. The church would be advertising a lie, and that would be wrong."

"Oh. I didn't think about that."

"Perhaps you should do a lot more thinking," said Mama.

7

"Go get into your costume, Anastasia," ordered Mrs. Pappas. "The photographer from the newspaper will be here any minute now." Stacy tried to protest, but Mrs. Pappas pushed her out of the hall and into the ladies restroom. "Don't talk. Change!"

"I'm going to tell Mrs. Pappas today," vowed Stacy, putting on her white stockings. "She'll understand. I just can't miss the girl scout trip."

She tugged the long-sleeved white blouse over her head and pulled the burgundy skirt up over her hips. It was gathered at the waist and had decorative gold braid around the bottom. The hem touched just below her knees. Stacy struggled into the short black jacket which had the same gold braid all around the edge and hooked a necklace of coins around her throat. She looked at her reflection in the mirror and put the burgundy scarf on her head and tied it behind her neck. The scarf hung half way down her back.

"Just like YiaYia's braid," thought Stacy, swinging her pretend hair. She clipped on the earrings which matched the necklace and went out to find Mrs. Pappas. What if Mrs. Pappas wouldn't listen again? What if she made Stacy pose for the picture? Another thought stabbed at Stacy. What if she wasn't doing the right thing?

People were rushing everywhere. Stacy had never seen so much activity. Father Nick came out of his office. He was dressed in his long black robe, and he smiled at her.

"Hello Anastasia," his voice boomed. "How beautiful you look in your costume."

"Thank you, Father," said Stacy, kissing the back of his hand quickly. She started to walk into the hall. Suddenly she remembered her dream. "Maybe I should ask Father Nick what to do?"

Father Nick had turned to go down the stairs as Stacy raced after him. "Father, can I talk to you?"

"Certainly," he said, taking her small hand in his. "I'm checking to see how everything is going. You can come tour with me. Panos is ready to raise the tent, and I saw your father out there, too."

"He brought me," said Stacy.

Stacy walked beside Father Nick as they headed out to the parking lot. Once a year the parking lot became a Greek village when the great blue and white tent went up. They passed people carrying tables, signs, and cooking equipment that would soon go under the tent. Father Nick and Stacy stopped at the edge of the lot.

Spread out on the ground lay the tent. There were three poles already standing in the ground with guide wires attached to the holes in the center of the tent. Panos was walking around the tent making sure it laid straight and would not snag on anything as it was pulled to the top of the poles. There were two men at every ten foot interval ready to pull the ropes at the edge of the tent. Once the tent was standing, one of the two men would attach the rope to a stake in the ground. Stacy watched in fascinated silence.

"Ready?" called Panos. One by one the men answered yes. "On my signal, everyone pull."

Panos raised his arm into the air and checked everything one more time. He dropped his arm and yelled, "Now!"

With a mighty tug on the ropes, the tent began to rise. Slowly it inched its way up the poles to the top. When it would go no further, one of the two men on each team hooked the looped ends of the ropes to the stakes pounded firmly into the ground while the other one held tightly to the rope. There was a yell as the last rope was secured, and workers pounded Panos on his back and shook his hand.

The sea of people parted to let Father Nick and Stacy pass through.

"Congratulations, Panos," said Father Nick, wrapping him in a big bear hug. "It's magnificent!"

"Thank you, Father. I couldn't have done it alone," declared Panos. He turned to his helpers and waved his cap. "Thank you all!"

The people who had been watching from the sidelines surged forward to prepare the food area, set up tables, and put out the signs. Father Nick and

41

Stacy looked on as the base for the barbecue spit was filled with sand. Here three whole lambs would be roasted at one time sending a mouth watering aroma through the tent. They would be served with the lemony Greek potatoes that Stacy loved.

Beside the lamb was the grill for frying the gyro meat. Stacy liked her gyros plain but most people preferred them wrapped in pita bread and smothered in sliced onions, tomatoes, and the traditional tzadziki sauce made from cucumbers and yogurt.

Next came souvlaki. The seasoned cubes of lamb on a stick were dipped in a lemon and oil sauce and then cooked on the grill. Stacy's stomach rumbled. This was Stacy's favorite and she could hardly wait to empty the stick onto the pita bread and take her first bite.

Father Nick and Stacy continued down the row where the visitors would choose their foods cafeteria style. Several men were struggling with two large metal shelf units.

"What are those?" asked Stacy.

"They're the warmers for the mousaka and the spanikopita," explained Father Nick. "They'll keep it nice and hot."

Stacy's mouth was watering. YiaYia made the best mousaka. First a layer of eggplant, then a layer of meat sauce, another layer of eggplant, and then the white sauce on top. Stacy remembered the first time she had seen an eggplant before it was cut. She had thought it looked like a giant grape.

The spanikopita was different. It used layers of

fillo on the top and bottom just like the baklava, but with only one thick layer of the spinach and cheese mixture in the middle.

Stacy watched as Father Nick helped her father roll the refrigerated case into place. This glass case would hold all the fixings for Greek salad. George's mother put the huge mixing bowl on the table.

"We're almost ready," she said.

Stacy and Father Nick continued their stroll around the tent. Everyone greeted them as they passed by.

"Where will they sell the pans of baklava, Father?" asked Stacy. "I made one."

"That's wonderful, Anastasia," complimented Father. "I think they'll be over here."

He led her across the tent, past the rows of tables being cleaned. There the ladies were setting up the glass cases for the pastries sold both individually and in bulk. Pans of baklava and dozens of cookies were already packaged in plastic containers. There were boxes and trays of pastries everywhere. Instructions flew back and forth in Greek and English.

"Ochi, ochi. No, no. Don't put that sign there. You'll block the entrance," shouted someone. "Over here. Put it over here."

"This is for you, Father Nick," said Stephanie's mother, handing the priest a piece of baklava. "One for you, too, Stacy."

They sat at one of the tables and watched the activity. Stacy had never seen any of this before. She was usually in school. When she came on Friday evening to dance, everything was already set up. She had never considered how it all got there. They finished their treats and deposited the napkins in the trash barrel.

"They're putting up the dance floor, Anastasia," said Father Nick. "Let's go see."

Stacy watched as the pieces of the dance floor were put together like a jigsaw puzzle. Panos checked to make sure that the edges fit tight.

"Can't have one of our beautiful dancers fall, now can we?" he said, kissing Stacy's forehead and hugging her to him. "Especially, my beautiful God-daughter."

"Maybe next year my Anna will start to dance," said Father. "Perhaps you will help her?" He smiled at Stacy as he stroked his beard.

Father Nick's little girl was in kindergarten this year and not old enough to learn the intricate dance steps. But next year she would be ready for Greek dancing and probably Greek language school, too.

"I'll teach her everything I know," said Stacy.

"You know, Anastasia, I'm always amazed that this festival comes together so well." Father Nick waved his arms in the direction of the tent and sighed. "There's so much work. The ladies have been baking for weeks. And you dancers. Practicing so hard." He hugged Stacy.

"Our people donate their time so we can raise money to help our church and bring a little bit of Greece to those people who may never see it any other way. I feel very fortunate to be part of such a community effort."

Father Nick stood straight and tall.

"Anastasia, I'm so proud of them! And proud of you, too!"

Stacy felt guilty. She wondered how proud Father Nick would be of her if he knew she was planning to desert her fellow dancers to go horseback riding in the mountains. Stacy watched him smile as they continued to wander around the tent. All the people were working so well together.

Stacy's father and Panos were laughing as they hung the signs showing the menu and the prices. She gasped as her father toppled off the ladder and landed on top of Panos.

"Thank you my friend for being such a soft cushion!" said Stacy's father, taking Panos' hand and pulling him to his feet.

"Next year you hold the ladder, Kosta," stated Panos. "It's better for a younger man to put up the signs!"

"Are those two at it again?" asked Mama, as Father Nick took the boxes of pastries from her arms and carried them over to the cases for her. "There isn't more than six months difference in their ages!"

"Their arguments are one of the best parts of the festival, Eleni," laughed Father Nick. He picked out two more pieces of baklava and handed one to Stacy. "And your baklava is another one!"

He popped the whole piece into his mouth.

"Without your pastries, Eleni, there would be no festival," said Father Nick, licking his fingers. "And that's a fact!"

"Oh, Father," scolded Mama, trying to replace her smile with a frown. But Stacy noticed that Mama was blushing.

"Let's go see how things are going inside at the import store," said Father Nick, taking Stacy's hand. "Your mama has everything under control out here!"

As they started into the hall, George ran up behind Stacy.

"You have to come now. Mrs. Pappas wants us to practice before the newspaperman gets here to take the pictures," he said and ran on to find the other dancers who were roaming through the tent.

"Anastasia, forgive me. Here I've been dragging you all over when you wanted to talk to me," said Father Nick.

"That's okay, Father," said Stacy. "I think I just answered my own question."

8

"Anastasia, here is the mantili," said Mrs. Pappas, giving her the white handkerchief. Stacy posed with her hand on her hip and whirled the mantili over her head.

"Smile," ordered the photographer and snapped the picture. "Just one more and we'll be done."

He placed the girls side by side behind the boys who were down on one knee in the front row.

"Now put your arms out as if you were finishing a number." He returned to the camera and adjusted the lens. "Good. Now say feta!" he instructed.

The minute the shutter clicked the dancers raced downstairs to change their clothes. The ladies bathroom was crowded.

"Do you need a ride tomorrow night?" asked Stephanie as she stepped out of her costume.

"If your mom wouldn't mind," Stacy answered without hesitation. "That way Mama could get here earlier and not have to wait for me to get home from school."

"We'll pick you up around 5:00," said Stephanie.

She placed her costume on the rack, hugged Stacy, and ran up the stairs.

"Thanks, Stephanie," called Stacy. "See you tomorrow."

Stacy was still in her costume, the mantili tucked in the waist of her skirt. She studied her reflection in the mirror and brushed away a tear that had escaped down her cheek.

"Everyone else is doing their job for the festival," she thought to herself and, standing straight and tall, she smiled. "I have to do my part, too. If everyone had something else to do, there wouldn't be a festival."

Stacy finished changing her clothes and headed up the stairs almost colliding with her mother. "Where's Papa?" she asked.

"He had to get back to the restaurant," said Mama.

"Are you done?" asked Stacy.

"For today." Mama looked tired. She sighed. "There's still a lot to do tomorrow."

"Stephanie's mom will pick me up tomorrow, so you can come early if you need to."

Mama raised her eyebrows. "You're going to dance?"

Stacy nodded.

"YiaYia will be so pleased," said Mama, quietly.

"I'm not dancing just for YiaYia, Mama," explained Stacy.

"I know," said Mama, putting her arm around Stacy's shoulders.

Stacy saw the crinkles form around her mother's eyes and the smile appear slowly on her face. Even though she didn't say so, Stacy figured Mama was pleased, too.

"There's just something about helping at the festival that makes you feel good," laughed Mama as they walked up the stairs. "Tired, but good."

YiaYia Sofia wasn't simply pleased. She was absolutely thrilled!

"I will come watch my Anastasia dance on Saturday," she stated.

"You had better call Mrs. Nelson and let her know you won't be going on the scout trip after all," said Mama as they sat down to dinner.

"I will, Mama."

Stacy, YiaYia, and Mama made the sign of the cross, touching thumb and first two fingers of the right hand to the forehead, chest, right shoulder, and left shoulder. With her right hand resting on her chest, Mama said the blessing.

After dinner Stacy cleared the table, and YiaYia washed the dishes. Stacy thought YiaYia must be feeling much better. She was dancing at the sink again.

"I've never seen the tent go up before," said Stacy as she dried a plate. "It was awesome!" She put the stack of plates in the cupboard. "YiaYia, did your village have a festival?"

"Oh yes! We had many festivals! Mostly for weddings, but other times, too. With lots of music and dancing and food. Such good times." YiaYia danced as she finished the dishes.

"Did you have a tent?"

"No, the church puts up the tent to make the village. We already had the village."

"Do you miss your village in Greece, YiaYia?"

"Sometimes." YiaYia Sofia took off her apron and hung it on the hook by the kitchen door. "But the Greek Festival brings my village to me, and that is nice."

She hugged Stacy as they walked into the living room together. Before going into her bedroom, YiaYia held Stacy's face in her hands and whispered.

"Sometimes it's hard to decide what is best to do when both things are good. Kalo Koritzi!" She tapped Stacy's nose with her finger. "Poli kalo! Kali nichta."

"Good night, YiaYia," said Stacy, laughing. She wasn't a naughty girl anymore. She was a very good girl.

The ladies bathroom at the church was packed with dancers as Stacy struggled into a corner beside Stephanie to change into her costume. Saturday and Sunday all three dance groups performed. Only Stacy's junior group had danced Friday night, but today they would lead each of the four sets followed by the beginning and senior groups.

"Hurry up, girls," commanded Mrs. Pappas. "It's almost time."

As Stacy led her group of dancers up the stairs, she thought about the scout troop. They would be at Mrs. Nelson's ranch by now. Maybe even going on a horseback ride. She wished that the festival and the trip had not been on the same weekend. She felt a twinge of regret, wondering if she had made the right decision.

As the music started, Stacy whirled the mantili above her head and holding George's hand, she led the dancers onto the stage. She turned inward toward the dancers and back out toward the audience as she guided the line of boys and girls around the floor. She noticed YiaYia Sofia sitting in the front row, beaming at her. Stacy smiled and held her head up high, and she knew this was the right place to be.

She saw her great grandmother nudge the lady next to her and point at Stacy.

"That's my great granddaughter," said YiaYia proudly. "She leads the dancers because she is the best one!"

The lady nodded in agreement and laughed. Stacy wondered if YiaYia knew the lady. She didn't recognize her. But then most of the people who came to the festival were strangers to Stacy. What had Father Nick said? 'It's good to bring a little bit of Greece to those who might never be able to go there.' Or something like that. So lots of people came to Greece for the day, to taste the food, watch the dancers, visit the church, and just have a good time.

They finished their first dance and lined up for the second. Stacy handed the mantili to Stephanie who would lead this one and took her place at the other end of the line.

"That was great, Stacy!" she heard someone yell.

She looked around the sea of faces. No one at church ever called her Stacy. There several rows back was Erin, standing and waving frantically. Stacy missed a step and stumbled. George's strong hand kept her from falling.

"Watch what you're doing," he hissed. "Not the audience!"

"Sorry," she apologized and looked over her shoulder at the place where she had seen Erin. Erin was sitting now, but Stacy recognized Mrs. Nelson and the rest of the girl scouts. She couldn't believe her eyes. What were they doing here? They were supposed to be in the mountains, riding horses!

When the second dance ended, the group bowed, and the audience applauded. The girls stepped back and clapped in time to the music while the boys took their turn. Then George moved to the center of the stage for his solo. He whirled and jumped, slapping the inside and outside of his white boots, and then kicked his legs high into the air. He did great turning leaps around the stage and landed on a chair placed in the middle of the dance floor. George did several high kicks, and then he somersaulted off the back of the chair!

There were gasps from people watching, and the girl scouts were clapping wildly. Stacy retrieved the mantili from Stephanie and steered the dancers off the stage and into the crowd as the beginning group went out onto the dance floor.

Stacy raced over to Erin. "You were great!" she exclaimed.

The scouts left their seats and gathered around Stacy.

"What a beautiful costume!"

"Uh, thanks, Allison," stammered Stacy.

"Can you teach us to do those dances?" asked Allison. "I think they'd be such fun to do at the Scout conference."

"You do?" squeaked Stacy.

"That's a wonderful idea," said Mrs. Nelson.

"I don't understand all this," said Stacy, trying to catch her breath. "I thought you were all going to the mountains."

"We couldn't go without you," said Mrs. Nelson. "When your great grandmother explained the situation and told me what a difficult decision you had to make, we took a vote."

"You talked to my YiaYia Sofia? When?"

"Yesterday. We had a very nice chat about you and horses and your commitment to the festival," explained Mrs. Nelson. "She invited us, so I called an emergency meeting, and we decided unanimously to come to the Greek Festival and go to the mountains next weekend."

Mrs. Nelson smiled at Mama who came to stand behind Stacy.

"Provided it's all right with your mother, of course."

"I think she'll be able to go," said Mama.

Stacy turned and threw her arms around her

mother's waist. "Thank you. Thank you."

"Don't thank me," said Mama, looking into Stacy's eyes. Mama smiled and then winked.

Stacy raced over to where her great grandmother was sitting. She hugged her tightly and knelt down beside her.

"Thank you for talking to Mrs. Nelson, YiaYia. She brought the whole scout troop." Stacy pointed to the area where the girls were standing. "They're over there. And guess what? They aren't going to the mountains until next weekend, and Mama said I could go!" Stacy hugged her again. "And it's all because of you. I love you, YiaYia!"

"You're not mad with me?" YiaYia Sofia patted Stacy's cheek.

"Oh no, YiaYia. Why would I be mad at you?"

"I meddle."

"I'm glad you meddled," said Stacy. She kissed YiaYia Sofia's cheek and hurried back to the scout group.

Erin quickly pulled her away. "Okay, friend. Who's the boy who danced by himself?"

"You mean George?"

"Yeah, George. Like where have you been hiding him?"

KALI ÓREXI!!

(Good Appetite)!!

STACY AND THE GREEK FESTIVAL

GLOSSARY

Anastasia	(A-nas-ta-sée-a)	Stacy's full name
Enas ipnothalamos	(É-nas ip-no-thál-a-mos)	A dormitory
Kafeneon	(Kaf-e-née-on)	Cafe
Kako koritzi	(Ka-kó kor-ít-zi)	Naughty girl
Kali nichta	(Ká-lee ních-ta)	Good night
Kalo koritzi	(Ka-ló kor-ít-zi)	Good girl
Koritzakimou	(Kor-it-zák-i-mu)	My girl (endearing)
Koritzimou	(Kor-ít-zi-mu)	My girl
Kumbara	(Kum-bá-ra)	Wedding attendant
Mantili	(Man-tí-li)	Handkerchief
Ochi	(Ó-khee)	No
Papou	(Pa-póo)	Grandfather
Pedakimou	(Pe-dák-i-mu)	My child (endearing)
Poli kalo	(Po-lée ka-ló)	Very good
Poli oraya	(Po-lée or-rá-ya)	Very beautiful
Signomi	(Sig-nó-mee)	Excuse me
Stephana	(Stéf-fa-na)	Wedding crowns
Thotheka ora	(Thó-thek-a ór-a)	Twelve o'clock
Ti enay ena	(Tee ée-nay é-na)	What is a
YiaYia	(Yá-Ya)	Grandmother

STACY AND THE GREEK FESTIVAL

GREEK FOODS

Baklava	(Bak-la-vá)	Honey/nut pastry
Briki	(Brée-kee)	Long handled brass or copper pot for making Greek coffee
Feta	(Fét-ta)	Goat cheese
Fillo	(Fée-lo)	Thin pastry sheets
Gyro	(Yée-ro)	Pita sandwich
Kafes	(Ka-fés)	Coffee
Kaimaki	(Ka-má-ki)	Light colored froth on Greek coffee
Mousaka	(Mu-sa-ká)	Eggplant casserole
Souvlaki	(Su-vlá-kee)	Meat shishkabob
Spanikopita	(Span-i-kóp-i-ta)	Spinach casserole
Tzadziki	(Tzad-zée-kee)	Sauce for gyro
Tsurekia	(Tsur-rék-i-a)	Braided sweet breads
Vassinada	(Vas-i-ná-da)	Cherry jam

ABOUT THE AUTHOR

Karen Papandrew is a Northwest transplant from the Arizona desert, actually preferring gray skies and rainy days to 100 degree heat and constant sunshine. "I love to curl up in front of a fire with a good book," she says.

This is Karen's first published novel, and several of her other novels and short stories have been contest winners.

She is a member of the Greek Orthodox Church of the Assumption in Seattle, WA where she says, "the Greek Festival is a tradition not to be missed! I love it! Kali Órexi!"